RACHEL and OBADIAH

The "Obadiah" Books
by Brinton Turkle

Thy Friend, Obadiah
Obadiah the Bold
The Adventures of Obadiah
Rachel and Obadiah

Copyright © 1978 by Brinton Turkle

Library of Congress Cataloging in Publication Data

Turkle, Brinton.   Rachel and Obadiah.

SUMMARY: Both Rachel and Obadiah want to earn some money
by carrying the news of the next ship's arrival to Nantucket.
[1. Nantucket, Mass.—Fiction.   2. Friends, Society of—Fiction]
I. Title.
PZ7.T847Rac 1978   [E]   77-15661   ISBN 0-525-38020-5

Published in the United States by E. P. Dutton, a Division
of Sequoia-Elsevier Publishing Company, Inc., New York

Published simultaneously in Canada by Clarke,
Irwin & Company Limited, Toronto and Vancouver

Editor: Ann Durell

Printed in the U.S.A.   First Edition
10 9 8 7 6 5 4 3 2 1

RACHEL
and
OBADIAH,

by
Brinton Turkle

E. P. Dutton   New York

It was a warm, sunny day on Nantucket Island. No one was stirring on India Street. But back of the old Pinkham house, Rachel and Obadiah Starbuck were busy picking blackberries.

Rachel's pail was almost full. Obadiah's pail was only half full.

"If thee eats all thy berries," Rachel told her brother, "Mother won't have enough for a pie."

Obadiah popped another big blackberry into his mouth. Juice trickled down his chin. "I'm not eating them all," he said. "Just some."

"Elizabeth! Elizabeth Woods!" Across the alley, Jessamy Morse was leaning out of her window, calling to her neighbor.

Elizabeth Woods raised her window and poked her head out.

"Has thee heard?" cried Jessamy Morse. "It's the *Clio*. She's at the bar! A boy brought Sarah Coffin the news. All well on board! Nathaniel is home safe; so is Abraham and thy Jabez, too. All safe!"

"Praise God!" said Elizabeth Woods. "I'll get the baby and see thee at the wharf."

Both windows banged shut.

Suddenly, all Nantucket was astir. The *Clio* had been to sea for more than a year. Everyone seemed to be running to greet her.

Rachel and Obadiah ran, too. They wiggled right up to the edge of the dock to watch the ship—her flags waving and sails billowing—come home.

Asa was showing something to his friends.

"What's that?" Obadiah asked his brother.

Asa held up a silver coin. "From the captain's wife," he said. "I was going by Jacob Slade's mill, when he runs up to me and says he's just sighted the *Clio* rounding the bar. He bids me run down to Captain Coffin's house with the news. And Sarah Coffin gives me this!"

Asa let Obadiah hold the money. It was new and very shiny.

Obadiah gave it back. "Does thee think Jacob Slade would ever send me with the news?" he said.

"The *Speedwell*'s due next week," said Asa. "I reckon he might, if thee is at his mill when he sights her."

At suppertime, Mother, Father, Moses, and Rebecca heard all about how Asa earned his prize.

Obadiah said, "Next week, the *Speedwell*'s coming in. I'm going up to the mill every day until Jacob Slade sights her."

"So am I," said Rachel.

"Thee!" Obadiah laughed. "He'd never send thee. Girls can't run. Not as fast as boys."

"We can, too!" said Rachel.

Mother said, "Girls can pick more blackberries than boys."

"I can *too* run fast," said Rachel. "Jacob Slade would send me, wouldn't he, Father?"

Father kissed Rachel and put her in her chair. "I know *I* would," he said. "I think Jacob Slade would, too."

The next day was First Day.

The Starbuck family were all at Meeting. So was Jacob Slade. After Meeting, Obadiah went up to him and said, "If I happened to be at thy mill and thee happened to sight a ship, would thee send me to the captain's house with the news?"

"Why, of course, lad. If thee is a good runner."

In a very tiny voice, Rachel said, "Would thee send me?"

"Well now," said the miller. "A girl's never carried the news. But I don't know why not."

"She can't run fast," said Obadiah.

"I can, too!" said Rachel.

Early the next day, Obadiah went right up to the mill. Rachel went right after him.

Jacob Slade scratched his chin. "Thee could have a mighty long wait," he said. "I don't know when the *Speedwell*'s coming in. Could be this week—or next. She might not even come in at all. Besides, how could I send both of you?"

Obadiah said, "We can have a race. We can run down to Pleasant Street, and back up Mill Street to Prospect. Thee could send the winner."

"Does that seem fair, Obadiah?" said the miller. "Rachel is smaller than thee."

"She can start first," said Obadiah.

After a moment, Jacob Slade said, "All right, if Rachel gets a head start."

"Get ready. Get set," said the miller. When he said "Go!" Rachel went.

Soon she was running down Pleasant Street. Someone was on the stoop of Grandmother Mitchell's house. It was Aunt Dorcas with a big basket. "My goodness, Rachel," she said. "Wherever is thee going in such a hurry?"

"A race," said Rachel. "I'm winning." And she kept on running.

Near Summer Street, Rachel heard footsteps pounding behind her. It was Obadiah. He caught up to her and ran a circle around her, showing off.

But, suddenly, Obadiah let out a whoop and dashed over to a field next to the Bunker house. "Blackberries!" he shouted. "Millions of them! I can pick a bushel and still catch up to thee!"

Rachel kept on running.

Turning into Mill Street, she caught her foot in her petticoat and fell down. Rachel began to cry. Why, oh why couldn't she wear britches like a boy?

A wagon creaked by. "Whoa!" said the driver. "What's the matter, little girl? Are you hurt?"

Rachel picked herself up and wiped her tears away with her fist. "No," she said. And she kept on running.

Ahead was Prospect Street. Behind, Obadiah was nowhere in sight.

Just over the top of the hill, getting nearer and nearer, were the vanes of Jacob Slade's windmill slowly turning.

Rachel kept on running.

Jacob Slade was waiting with a big smile on his face. "Thee's won!" he exclaimed. "Good for thee, Rachel Starbuck!"

Was it true? Had she really won? Where was Obadiah?

The miller said, "Does thee think thee can run any farther?"

Rachel nodded her head. "I can run *much* farther," she said.

Jacob Slade took her by the hand. "Let me show thee something," he said.

"Look yonder. Out by Brant Point."

"A ship!" said Rachel. "Is she . . . ?"

"The *Speedwell*!" said the miller. "She's early. See her flags? They show all's well aboard. Does thee think thee can run to Captain Hussey's house with the good news?"

"Yes," said Rachel. "Oh, yes!"

Lydia Hussey wiped her eyes and blew her nose. "I dreamed the *Speedwell* was lost at sea," she said. "Praise the Lord that wasn't true."

The captain's wife gave Rachel a hug, then went to her cupboard and pulled out a brass box from behind a blue teapot. She took a silver coin from the box and gave it to Rachel.

"Thank thee, dear child," she said.

She put on her shawl and bonnet. Then she began to cry all over again. " 'All well on board,' did thee say?"

Lydia Hussey got another coin from the box and pressed it into Rachel's hand. "Bless thee, Rachel Starbuck. Thee brings the gladdest tidings."

Rachel got another hug and a rather wet kiss.

Once again, all Nantucket was astir.

Rachel stood at the gate of Captain Hussey's house, looking at the two beautiful pieces of silver. Whatever would she do with two of them?

Down the street came Obadiah. Blackberry juice was all over his face, and he looked very angry.

Rachel put one coin in her pocket. She would keep it forever.

And she knew just what to do with the other one.